An Alaska Counting Rhyme

Sara Feriante Donkersloot
Illustrated by Dale C. Preston

PO Box 221974 Anchorage, Alaska 99522-1974

Manufactured in Hong Kong

ISBN 1-888125-60-8

Library of Congress Catalog
Card Number: 99-067475

Copyright 1999 by
Sara Feriante Donkersloot

—First Edition—

All rights reserved, including the right of
reproduction in any form, or by any mechanical
or electronic means including photocopying or
recording, or by any information storage or
retrieval system, in whole or in part in any
form, and in any case not without the
written permission of the author and publisher.

Dedication

For the children of Alaska. The next time you go for a walk or a boat ride down by the river, see if *you* can spot any of the animals pictured here. Watch closely ... some of them are sure to be there!

Acknowledgments

With thanks to the elementary staff at Bristol Bay Borough School in Naknek, Loretta Smith at the Martin Monsen Library, King Salmon Visitor's Center, King Salmon offices of Fish and Wildlife and National Park Service, retired Fish and Game Supervisor Richard Russell, and Ms. Feriante's kindergarten class of 1998-99.

Down by the river where the cool waters run
Lived an old mother moose and her little calf one.
"Browse," said the mother.
"I browse," said the one.
And they browsed on the grass where the cool waters run.

Down by the river under skies so blue
Lived an old mother eagle and her little eaglets two.
"Flap," said the mother.
"We flap," said the two.
And they flapped their wings under skies so blue.

Down by the river near the aspen tree
Lived an old mother bear and her little cubs three.
"Fish," said the mother.
"We fish," said the three.
And they fished all day near the aspen tree.

Down by the river where the fast waters roar
Lived an old mother otter and her little pups four.
"Slide," said the mother.
"We slide," said the four.
And they slid and they splashed where the fast waters roar.

Down by the river where the wild iris thrive
Lived an old mother fox and her little kits five.
"Pounce," said the mother.
"We pounce," said the five.
And they pounced and they chased where the wild iris thrive.

Down by the river in a lodge made of sticks
Lived an old mother beaver and her little kits six.
"Gnaw," said the mother.
"We gnaw," said the six.
And they gnawed and they built their lodge made of sticks.

Down by the river in their safe quiet haven
Lived an old mother hare and her little leverets seven.
"Hop," said the mother.
"We hop," said the seven.
And they hopped and they rested in their safe quiet haven.

Down by the river where the grass grew straight
Lived an old mother wolf and her little pups eight.
"Play," said the mother.
"We play," said the eight.
And they played in the moonlight where the grass grew straight.

Down by the river where the blue waters shine
Lived an old mother swan and her little cygnets nine.
"Paddle," said the mother
"We paddle," said the nine.
And they paddled all around where the blue waters shine.

Down by the river in a dark rocky den
Lived an old mother mink and her little kits ten.
"Run," said the mother.
"We run," said the ten.
And they ran and they hid in their dark rocky den.

Baby Animal Facts

Moose calves are born in May and June each year. At birth, the calves weigh only 25 to 35 pounds. They spend several months feeding on their mother's milk, but are soon eating grass and other plants. After only five months a baby moose weighs almost 400 pounds. Until they are big enough to run with their mothers, moose calves are easy prey for wolves and bears. Moose mothers, called cows, hide their new calves in thick bushes. If an enemy gets too close to the calf, the moose cow protects the calf by kicking with her sharp hooves.

Eaglets are very ugly and small at birth. They weigh only three ounces, are covered with down instead of feathers, and their heads seem much too big for their scrawny bodies. The newborns are too weak to stand because the effort of breaking out of the egg completely exhausts them. For the first week the parents still keep them warm. The father does most of the hunting for the mother and the young. He brings prey back to the nest where the mother uses her hooked beak to shred it and feed it to the eaglets. The young eaglets eat almost as much food as their parents.

From one to four cubs are born to the mother bear in the den in January. They are small and only weigh about one pound. Their eyes are closed and they are covered with fine hair. The cubs spend the time till spring fattening up on their mother's milk and weigh about seven pounds when they leave the den for the first time. Play is important for the cubs because it helps them sharpen their skills so they wrestle and tumble and chase each other. Cubs watch their mother to learn what foods are good to eat and how to look out for danger.

Otter pups are born with their eyes closed and no teeth. They feed on the mother's milk. When the pups are big enough to leave the den, the father otter may join the family and help teach the pups how to swim, slide, dive, and catch food. Pups don't swim until they're several months old, but they are able to close their ears and nostrils when they are under water. As the pups grow bigger they learn to catch and eat fish. River otter pups are playful and like to slide down muddy slopes in the spring and play in the snow in the winter.

The mother fox, or vixen, has her kits in the early spring. The babies weigh less than four ounces and are able to open their eyes after about nine days. Then the father fox is sometimes allowed into the den. If not, he stays outside and stands guard or hunts for food to leave at the den entrance. The kits feed on their mother's milk for about five weeks and need to nurse about five times a day. They start to get their first teeth at about three weeks. The kits leave the den when they are a month old. Their parents teach them how to hunt for food like mice and hares.

Beaver kits are born with fur on and their eyes already open. Some teeth have already appeared and they are nursing within the hour. The kits can swim when they are only a few days old. By the time they are two weeks old, the young beavers weigh almost two pounds and are ready to follow their parents out of the lodge and begin feeding on whatever plants the older beavers are eating. A beaver kit can be easy prey for an otter, fish, or owl. Beavers warn each other of danger by slapping the surface of the water with their tails. Aspen trees are their favorite food.

Baby hares are called leverets. They are born furred and with their eyes already open. A mother may have three litters of leverets in just one summer. Hares eat grass, buds, twigs, and leaves. They are most active at night and rest during the day. Hares may thump the ground with their hind foot to warn others of nearby danger. Their fur is dark brown in the summer but changes to white in the winter. Hares always remain close to their home and usually don't travel more than a quarter mile from their birthplace.

Wolf pups are born in a den or cave in March or April. The newborn pups are blind and deaf. In a few days they are able to hear and then in about two weeks their eyes open. It takes about a month before their floppy ears will stand up. Wolves live in family groups called packs and both the mother and father help to raise the pups. The adults teach the young pups how to hunt. In midsummer the pups will leave the den with their parents and start to travel and hunt with the pack.

Both the male and female swan help to build their large nest. They make it mostly of plant material and it is usually out in the open and easy to see. The baby swans, called cygnets, can see and swim as soon as they hatch. They are quick to leave the nest and when only one day old are able  to follow their parents to look for food. It takes less than three months for the cygnet to grow from a six-ounce ball of down into a ten-pound juvenile swan. Young swans stay with their parents for almost a year and may fly with them when they migrate south for the winter.

Baby mink are called kits. They are born in mid-June in a nest lined with fur, feathers, and dry plants. Kits are four or five inches long and are covered with short, fine, light colored hair. They are blind and naked at birth. The young kits' eyes don't open 'till they are about five weeks old, but even with their eyes closed they are able to chew on meat that is brought to  the den by the father and mother. Once their eyes open, they are weaned and live entirely on meat. Mink hunt well on land but are also good swimmers. You don't often see a mink because they are most active at night.

Plants Shown in Down by the River

Page 4
  spruce
  lupine
Page 5
  aspen
  fireweed
Page 8
  fireweed
  buttercup
  high bush cranberry
Page 9
  wild iris
  aspen
Page 11
  salmon berry

Page 12-13
  wild iris
  toadstool

Page 14-15
  aspen
Page 16-17
  wild rose
  forget me not
  lupine
Page 18-19
  cattail
Page 20-21
  water lily
  cattail
Page 22-23
  blueberry
  spruce

Insects

There are bees and butterflies on many of the pages.
Can you find them?

Additional Animals

Page 4
  caribou
Page 8
  hare
Page 9
  tree squirrel
Page 10
  porcupine
Page 11
  tree squirrel
Page 13
  field mice
Page 14
  moose

Page 15
  bear
  tree squirrel
  hare
Page 16
  parkie squirrel
Page 18
  mink
Page 21
  beaver
Page 22
  bear
Page 23
  tree squirrel

Geography

Page 4-5
  Katmai Range
  Naknek River
Page 6-7
  Naknek River
  (note the glacier)
Page 18-19
  Mt. Katolinat by
  the Valley of Ten Thousand Smokes

Page 20-21
  Mt. Dumpling
  in Katmai
  National Park
Page 22-23
  Brooks Falls on
  the Brooks River
  in Katmai
  National Park

Birds

Page 5
  raven
Page 6
  downy woodpecker
Page 8
  snow bunting
Page 9
  hummingbird
Page 11
  Western sandpiper
Page 12
  Canadian geese

Page 14
  magpie
  mallard duck
Page 16
  tundra swans
Page 21
  mallard duck
Page 22
  ptarmigan
Page 23
  snowy owl

Fish

Page 8
  sockeye salmon
  rainbow trout
  grayling
Page 9
  humpy
Page 10
  arctic char
  sockeye salmon

Page 11
  silver salmon
Page 18
  chum salmon
  sockeye salmon
Page 19
  king salmon
  silver salmon
Page 23
  silver salmon

Down by the River

1. Down by the river where the cool waters run, Lived an old mother moose and her little calf one. "Browse," said the mother. "I browse," said the one. And they browsed on the grass where the cool waters run.

Down by the river under skies so blue
Lived an old mother eagle and her little eaglets two.
"Flap," said the mother.
"We flap," said the two.
And they flapped their wings under skies so blue.

Down by the river near the aspen tree
Lived an old mother bear and her little cubs three.
"Fish," said the mother.
"We fish," said the three.
And they fished all day near the aspen tree.

Down by the river where the fast waters roar
Lived an old mother otter and her little pups four.
"Slide," said the mother.
"We slide," said the four.
And they slid and they splashed where the fast waters roar.

Down by the river where the wild iris thrive
Lived an old mother fox and her little kits five.
"Pounce," said the mother.
"We pounce," said the five.
And they pounced and they chased where the wild iris thrive.

Down by the river in a lodge made of sticks
Lived an old mother beaver and her little kits six.
"Gnaw," said the mother.
"We gnaw," said the six.
And they gnawed and they built their lodge made of sticks.

Down by the river in their safe quiet haven
Lived an old mother hare and her little leverets seven.
"Hop," said the mother.
"We hop," said the seven.
And they hopped and they rested in their safe quiet haven.

Down by the river where the grass grew straight
Lived an old mother wolf and her little pups eight.
"Play," said the mother.
"We play," said the eight.
And they played in the moonlight where the grass grew straight.

Down by the river where the blue waters shine
Lived an old mother swan and her little cygnets nine.
"Paddle," said the mother
"We paddle," said the nine.
And they paddled all around where the blue waters shine.

Down by the river in a dark rocky den
Lived an old mother mink and her little kits ten.
"Run," said the mother.
"We run," said the ten.
And they ran and they hid in their dark rocky den.

The tune to *Down by the River* is from an old English song. Lyrics are by Sara Donkersloot using animals found along Alaska's many rivers, and is based on Olive A. Wadsworth's classic nursery poem, *Over in the Meadow*, written in the late 1800s.